A Rex Graves Mini-Mystery

SAY GOODBYE

~ TO ~

ARCHIE

C.S CHALLINOR

D1528302

Second Edition

Book cover, design, and production by Perfect Pages Literary Management, Inc.

ISBN-13: 978-1492131069
ISBN-10: 1492131067

DEDICATION

For Othello, the inspiration for this story, and also Fred, Tux, and Twinkie.

BOOK TITLES

REX GRAVES MYSTERY SERIES, PUBLISHED BY
MIDNIGHT INK BOOKS:

Christmas Is Murder
Murder in the Raw
Phi Beta Murder*
Murder on the Moor
Murder of the Bride
Murder at Midnight
Murder Comes Calling (2015)

PUBLISHED BY PERFECT PAGES LITERARY
MANAGEMENT, INC.:

Murder at the Dolphin Inn

~SAY GOODBYE TO ARCHIE~

* * *

*It is with a heavy heart that I write to inform you that
Archie passed away in the early hours of this morning.
A small ceremony will be held at the Poplars
on Saturday at four.
RSVP*

"You must go, Reginald," Rex's mother said in her genteel Edinburgh dialect. Summer rain spattered the panes behind the net curtains of the front parlour, where they were taking tea. "Archie meant the world to Patricia. And you know I can't travel that far."

"Even if we went down by train?"

His mother was terrified of public transport, but driving hundreds of miles in a car proved even more of a problem for her. Rex really didn't want to go by himself. He didn't want to go at all.

Patricia Forsyth was a batty old lady, a boarding school chum of his mother's from before the advent of television. His mother had had him late in life, as had Patricia her own two children.

"No, son, you go on my behalf. I'll telephone Patricia with my regrets."

"How old was Archie?"

"Eighteen. A good age for a cat. But that won't help ease her grief. He was her muse and constant companion, her reason for being."

"She has two children, doesn't she?"

"Constance and Charles," his mother supplied, buttering a scone.

"I met them once at a funeral." Rex hadn't been very taken with them, but then funerals were not the best places to form opinions of people, he supposed.

"In the last letter I received from Patricia, Archie was in fine form and had received a clean bill of health from the veterinary surgeon. So his sudden death has come as a tragic shock to her."

"Aye, it's hard to believe he's gone," Rex commiserated, helping himself to another cup of tea.

Archie was an institution. He had featured under an alias in so many illustrated children's books Rex had lost count. There had been *Claude the Narcissistic Cat, Claude the Contemplative Cat, Claude the Inquisitive Cat, Claude the Clandestine Cat, Claude the Comedic Cat*, and the list had gone on.

Patricia Forsyth, an erstwhile teacher of English at a girls' private school in Edinburgh, had retired to the warmer climes of the south coast of England, where she lived in a village outside of Eastbourne. Inspired by Archie, she had dreamt up the Claude the Cat series to instruct precocious young children in the use of polysyllabic adjectives. Claude was a multifaceted cat who partook of various adventures reinforcing the meaning of the (insert) descriptive word in the title. The series had become highly popular and lucrative, helped by the winsome portrayal of Claude in elegantly stylized illustrations, not dissimilar to *le Chat Noir* immortalised in posters advertising the late nineteenth century cabaret of that name in Montmartre. By virtue of her beloved pet, Patricia had helped develop the vocabulary of tens of thousands of children in English-speaking countries as far away as New Zealand.

Rex's mother dabbed at her lips with the white linen napkin. "Patricia said on the phone she feels she can never write another Archie story again." Everyone knew her all-black, medium-haired domestic breed had served as the model for Claude.

Rex wondered how many alliterative titles could have been left. "Perhaps now she can round off the series with *Claude the Cremated Cat.*" His facetiousness derived mainly from his irritation at having to go all the way to the Sussex coast to attend a pet's ceremony; not that he was not sympathetic to Patricia's loss.

His mother, a snowy-haired and tight-lipped lady, dainty as a china doll, *tsked-tsked* at him across the table.

Rex gave a sigh of contrition. "Don't think I'm not saddened by Archie's death. I remember him well even though it's been years. And don't worry," he consoled his mother. "Archie will live on in the books. Patricia Forsyth will be remembered along with Michael Bond and Beatrix Potter, and whoever wrote those stories about Babar the Elephant."

"But Patricia is not as concerned about immortality as the here and now. She got Archie when her husband died, and he was a great solace to her. All she ever talked aboot was Archie and his latest escapade, although lately it was more his state of health. A stiffness in his joints, his getting more fussy aboot his food, that sort of thing. But nothing major."

Getting on was no fun for man or beast, Rex reflected, himself middle-aged and showing the signs around his mid-section.

His mother shook her head sadly. "She'll be at a complete loss now."

"Perhaps getting another cat to replace him would help?"

"Och, noo!" she protested. "Patricia would

never think of it. It would seem like a betrayal. And what makes it worse is she thinks he was murdered!"

Rex choked on a crumb from his scone. "Murdered?" he finally got out. He washed his throat down with tea.

"By someone in the village."

Rex eyed his mother over the rim of his cup. Now he fully understood her insistence that he travel down to the Poplars in Woodley. He was expected to solve the mystery of a murdered cat! An allegedly murdered cat. Patricia Forsyth was not only batty but evidently possessed of a morbidly vivid imagination. He was, in effect, being assigned the role of pet detective. He gazed insistently at his mother demurely sipping her tea.

"Well, you needn't look so cross, Reginald. It's not as though you had anything important planned for the weekend."

"That's the whole point! I was planning to take the weekend off and relax with a good book. It's been an exceptionally busy week in court and I was hoping to get a break from murders, even those of a feline nature." He had a sudden thought. "Archie was killed by another cat, right? Or a dog? He got in a fight or was chased into the road and run over by a car?"

"Noo," his mother exclaimed. "Patricia said he was poisoned. So the question is, who would wish him dead? I told her you'd be the one to find

7

oot. You can take your book wi' you on the train," she said with finality.

Their housekeeper had cut a few slices of Battenberg cake bought from Marks & Spencer's. Miss Bird didn't bake as much now that her eyesight was failing. Too much salt had been inadvertently substituted for sugar on many an occasion with disastrous results. Rex cut a piece into four pink and yellow squares and began by licking off the marzipan.

"Och, Reggie, ye did that when ye were a bairn." Miss Bird chuckled as she sat down to join them as she habitually did at the end of her work day.

Only at home was he called Reggie and Reginald, detestable names both. As soon as he started Latin in school and learned the declension of the noun "king," the origin of his name, he had contrived to go by Rex. But Miss Bird apparently still saw the bulky redhead as a lad in short trousers. He wiped his mouth with the starched napkin and brushed away any crumbs on his beard.

"I suppose I had better pack for my trip," he said pointedly. "See an old lady aboot a cat," he explained to Miss Bird.

"Patricia will be so glad to see you, Reginald. She always said I had the prince of sons."

His mother could be very manipulative. "I hope you did not raise her hopes, Mother. It'll be hard, if not impossible, to prove anyone poisoned Archie."

"I forgot to tell you! Patricia received a note through her letterbox. It was composed of capital letters cut out of a newspaper. Can ye credit it?" she asked Miss Bird. "This was the day before he was murdered. It said, 'SAY GOODBYE TO ARCHIE'!"

*

Rex sat thoughtfully on the early morning train headed south from Waverley Station to Kings Cross in London. In spite of earlier reservations regarding the trip, he felt somewhat heartened by the news of the note. At least now he had a tangible piece of evidence to work with. The first clue. Hopefully, Patricia had kept the note. He wondered if she had shown it to the police and, if so, whether they had taken it seriously. And why not a ransom note instead? Patricia was well off. Abducting the cat and demanding money for its return would have been less callous, relatively speaking, and he felt sure Patricia would have paid up. Obviously the motive for murdering Archie had not been monetary. So what had it been? Spite? Envy?

He continued to ponder. Would reporters be at her home? He supposed he would have to ask her the usual questions in such a situation: Did

Archie have any enemies? Was he acting strangely before his death? Cats had a premonition about death, he had heard. Patricia might have noticed Archie reacting in a negative way towards a particular individual. All these thoughts ran through his brain as fast as the dreary fields and hedgerows streaming past the window as he drank the mediocre coffee provided courtesy of Network Rail. He would get the Eastbourne train from Victoria Station, arriving in Woodley in the early afternoon. How he was supposed to wrap up the case of a murdered muse in two days was the more puzzling mystery as far as he was concerned.

A vista of saffron yellow fields opened up beyond the tracks. The rapeseed in flower, much admired by Japanese tourists, looked artificial against the green countryside. Rex did not feel kindly towards this interference with the landscape. Hopefully, the village of Woodley had retained its traditional charm since he last visited the Poplars with his mother a decade ago. He unfolded the *Guardian* on his lap and began to read the newsprint, reaching into the pocket of his jacket for his spectacles. He had not needed these a decade ago.

His thoughts kept drifting back to the case of the murdered cat and what, if anything, the weekend might reveal. The sinister note could have been an unfortunately timed practical joke and coincidental to the alleged poisoning. He retained a few signed copies of the early Claude books at the Morningside house, gifts to his son when Campbell was nine or ten; when his wife was still alive, and before he took silk and became a QC. Seemed like a lifetime ago. He felt a stab of pain for Patricia Forsyth. She'd had Archie for eighteen years, longer than he had known Fiona, who had died of breast cancer. He seemed to remember Patricia had rescued Archie from a cat shelter on the advice of her doctor when she was mourning the loss of her husband. Archie had been a young cat then, not much more than a kitten. How cruel of someone to deprive her of one extra year or more of his life; if, in fact, the cat had been murdered. It seemed a bit far-fetched, in his opinion. He had called his fiancée to tell her about his latest private case and she'd been hugely amused, in spite of a natural empathy for the old lady.

Helen was a student counsellor and had a degree in psychology. He wished he could have taken the opportunity to visit her in Derby while he was in England, but she was attending a weekend course in Manchester.

"Well, this is a new departure for you, Rex, I must say," she had said the previous night. "But I hope you catch Archie's killer. People who kill animals often progress to murdering people."

*

Patricia had offered to send a friend to meet Rex off the train, but he had said on the phone he would avail himself of a taxi. Woodley was but a short drive from Eastbourne, a Victorian seaside resort that had seen better days. Yet, viewing the village of Woodley again after so many years, he found it barely changed. The white manor house stood on a hill lording it over the other residences, stone and brick homes and converted barns, nestled in a valley surrounded by woods, with the one road leading through to a dead end in front of the Poplars—so named for a line of such trees fronting the property, which at present waved in the soft breeze. He paid the cab fare and pushed open the black wrought-iron gate, which he noticed did not have a lock, and strolled with his overnight bag up the path cutting through the lawn to the front door. This was painted green to match the trim of the cottage. He rang the bell and the door opened almost instantaneously.

"Reginald, my dear boy! Come in." Patricia Forsyth was large-boned and still hearty for her octogenarian years. Her white hair had apparently not been acquainted with a pair of scissors in several days and stuck out every which way, and her spectacles sat askew on her nose. "So glad you made good time. That will give us an hour or so to sit and chat before the others arrive for tea." Her voice attested to her Scottish heritage. "Did you have lunch?" she enquired.

"I grabbed a sandwich at the station in London."

"On to business then."

She led him slowly down the hall into a back sitting room, which was as chaotic in aspect as its owner, with too much mismatched furniture and barely a free space on any elevated surface. Rex bowed his head beneath the low ceiling beams. The net curtains drawn across the bay window overlooked the back garden, which he could only perceive as a square of diffused green with a few splodges of colour, resembling a child's picture. There was no air conditioning in the cottage, and probably no need for an old person who invariably felt the cold regardless of temperature. Patricia wore an un-ironed blouse, a tweed jacket and skirt, stout shoes, and thick nylon stockings that failed to hide her bulging varicose veins.

"My digging shoes," she said in answer to his gaze. "For later."

Presumably she was referring to Archie's interment. Rex, for his part, divested himself of his jacket and, having seen nowhere to hang it, draped it over the arm of the chintz-covered sofa, which Archie had clearly abused as a scratching post.

"Reginald, it's so very good of you to come." Patricia took both his hands in her knotty ones and looked hypnotically up at his face through her eye-magnifying lenses. "You haven't changed. Perhaps a bit heavier. You look well."

"You too, Patricia. Or, at least, as well as can be expected under the sad circumstances." He handed her the condolence card from his mother.

Patricia shifted a heap of books and magazines to one side of the sofa and indicated for him to sit down. She smoothed the white envelope in her lap without making a move to open it. "Dear Moira. So thoughtful." She gave a deep sigh. "This will only make me cry," she said, finally placing it on a cluttered table where a tray held a pitcher full of ice and yellow liquid, and two beakers.

"Lemonade," she said pouring him a glass. "We'll have tea in the garden later, but for now it's more private inside. My neighbour is pottering about out there and he might overhear us. Now, before they all arrive, we should discuss the matter of Archie. I won't let his murder go unpunished. It was a heartless thing to do. To him and to me." Patricia pulled a crumpled handkerchief from her jacket pocket and blew her nose into it. "I can't live on here in Woodley always wondering which person committed the crime."

"You think it was someone local?"

"Sure of it. It's a small village and I've questioned everybody. No one recalls seeing a stranger this past week. Believe me, they'd know."

"Well, that limits the pool of suspects to under twenty or so," Rex said encouragingly.

"Seventeen," Patricia corrected. "And some of the residents can be ruled out. Mr. Davis is confined to a wheelchair. Madeline Squire at the B&B would have no reason to curtail poor Archie's life. She has quite a few guests who come to Woodley in part because I live here and the children like to get a glimpse of Archie. He was quite obliging. Sat grooming himself in the front window so they could see him and take his picture."

A portrait photo of Archie encased in a wreath stood on the piano. His long snout lent him a regal mien, softened by eyes as round as marbles and the hue of chartreuse gazing out from black fur. A silver bell dangled from his collar. Archie had allowed him to pet him on that visit ten years ago, and Rex had marvelled at how soft and sleek he was; soot black from his nose to his paw pads. A good size too, tufty-eared and bushy-tailed. Patricia had sworn he had some Maine Coon in him, but couldn't be sure.

"Could a child have done it?" Rex asked.

Patricia resolutely shook her head. "The only kids who live here took off to France with their parents for the summer hols."

"Did Archie have any enemies?" There, he had said it.

"Everyone loved Archie! Except perhaps

Noel Cribben."

Rex gave her a questioning look.

"The neighbour."

He took a sip of the bitter-sweet lemonade and waited to hear more about this Noel Cribben.

"You'll meet him this afternoon. His dog got into my garden and received a scratch on his nose for his efforts. Noel swore it was Archie who'd attacked him and wanted me to pay the vet bill. Of course, I refused. Cutie Pie shouldn't have been in my garden in the first place. Isn't that a ghastly name? He went on a rampage in my bed of delphiniums, snapping the blooms in two. Ruined half of them and dug a big hole. Fortunately, Archie chased him off before he could do more damage. He was only defending his territory, which is what cats do. I didn't see the actual altercation, just heard the growling and howling. By the time I got to the garden, the poodle had gone. Just as likely he cut his nose on some barbed wire. Noel couldn't prove Archie had actually attacked him."

"How did, ehm, Cutie Pie get in? I seem to remember your back garden is surrounded by a wall. Did he jump over?"

"I should say not!" Patricia seemed almost amused. "Not on those short legs. Q-P is a miniature poodle. Part of the wall had crumbled and he must have managed to clamber over. It's been mended, and there have been no further doggie incursions."

"If Archie was poisoned—"

"He was. Dr. Strange, our vet, found chopped foxglove in the contents of Archie's stomach and in his bowl." Patricia's tensely clenched knuckles whitened to the colour of the hankie she was holding. "Digitalis. Deadly poisonous. He didn't stand a chance."

A phone rang in the hall, but she took no notice. Was she hard of hearing? She didn't wear an aid that Rex could see, although it was hard to tell behind the wild tufts of hair. She certainly didn't appear to have difficulty hearing his questions.

"Foxglove is a common enough flower," he said.

"Oh, yes, it's all over the village."

"Presumably, it was mixed in with cat food."

"In Archie's tinned tuna. He began to get rather picky about his food and, naturally, I indulged him. After all he had done for me..." Her words ended in a sob and her hands trembled in her lap, but she found the fortitude not to break down.

"I kept his food bowl in the conservatory. I had that put in since your last visit. It doesn't have any windows or an exterior door. As for the rest of the house, I used to live in a city and never got into the habit of keeping my doors unlocked like some of my neighbours. In any case, I don't like the idea of someone coming in and snooping at my unfinished manuscripts. Or typescripts, I should say. It's not really a manuscript, is it, if it isn't written by hand? But I suppose that's being pedantic. It's old age, you know. You start obsessing over little things."

"What aboot a cleaning lady or someone visiting here? And on that note, I really would be fine at the B&B, you know."

"Nonsense. I told Moira I wouldn't hear of it. Charles and Connie are staying over, and it will be a bit snug, but Charles can sleep on the sofa."

"No, really—"

"I insist. You're the guest, and you came all the way from Edinburgh to help me find out who murdered my Archie. You can have Charles' old room."

"Och, I would not dream of throwing him oot his own room," Rex said, aghast at the thought.

"A night on the sofa won't hurt him. He's not as busy as you are. I was so proud when you became a Queen's Counsel. Perhaps Charles should have gone into law. His business is floundering. He won't admit it, but I know from Connie and the stress he's obviously under. No head for figures has Charles. Always was a dunce at arithmetic. You don't need it to practise law, do you?"

"Not as much as for business, I imagine."

"Well, good. That's settled."

Rex was not quite sure what had been settled, but he assumed it to be the sleeping arrangements; and he knew better than to broach the subject with Patricia again. She was a woman who knew her own mind. He would apologize to Charles when the opportunity arose.

"Where are Charles and Connie?" he asked. "I'm looking forward to seeing them again." He was not, particularly. However, he was curious as to their whereabouts. He had not heard anybody else in the cottage.

"They went for a hike to Alfriston. I make Charles walk every day when he visits. He's very sedentary."

Rex imagined Charles in a permanent sitting posture.

"And Connie needs the exercise too. She never lost the weight after her two children. They're with Nigel for the weekend. They get shunted from pillar to post like a pair of parcels!" Patricia set her mouth in a grim line. She had no doubt been a formidable school mistress in her day, feared by pupils and parents alike, and probably by the other teachers as well.

Attempting to get the conversation back on course, Rex repeated his earlier question about whether anyone came in to clean. Not that the house looked like it received a regular clean. All the clutter would have to be moved first, a

Herculean task in itself. "Such a person would have ready access to Archie's food," he suggested.

"Faye comes every other week. She didn't come this past week. No one was here the night Archie died. Apart from the killer, I mean. Anyway, Faye would never have hurt Archie. She was fond of him, as we all were."

Someone wasn't, Rex thought.

"And she knew that if I went before Archie, she was to live at the Poplars and take care of him for as long as he lived, and would be amply compensated."

"I see." Rex took a moment to ponder the situation. "I take it she was not averse to the arrangement when you discussed it with her?"

"She was delighted. She lives higgledy-piggledy with numerous siblings and a ne'er-do-well father in Eastbourne."

"Does she receive a gratuity under the current sad circumstances?"

"A small sum, as does the gardener and a few close friends."

"It might be as well to review the terms of your will to see if anyone benefits from Archie's death…"

Patricia topped up their lemonade glasses. Most of the ice had melted by now. A breeze blowing in through the window helped with the heat, but not much. "It's a natural question in a murder case, isn't it? Even though it wasn't my murder. Although I need to tell you about that, too. But later." She gazed into the contents of her glass and resumed speaking before he had a chance to ask what she meant. "Apart from gratuities to my help, I have bequeathed the same sum of three thousand pounds each to my friend Dot Sharpe and Roger Dalrymple, my illustrator. My library also goes to Dot. My piano I've left to Roger. Neither of my children ever got the hang of it. And my property and the remainder of the contents are to be split between Connie and Charles, who receive twenty thousand pounds each. The rest of my money goes to the cat orphanage in Eastbourne where I adopted Archie." She supplied a few further details. "No one benefits from Archie's death, really. Only from mine."

"Who has a key to this place?"

"My daughter. She insisted. She lives in Eastbourne and runs over when she has time, to check up on me in case I have a fall or I take ill. Charles has one too."

"Do any of your friends have a spare key in case of an emergency?"

Patricia paused for a moment. "You're right," she said slowly. "Dot has a house key. I gave it to her when I was away on a book tour so she could feed Archie. I'd forgotten to ask for it back."

"She's a good friend, I take it, since you've remembered her in your will?"

"Well, we'll have to see. She lives in the village, up by the manor house. Moved here about three years ago. She organizes our little book club."

"Retired?"

"Oh, by a long chalk. She's writing her memoirs. A tough sell unless you're somebody famous."

"Has she got a story to tell?"

"Dashed if I know. I've only seen a few excerpts of her work. She did grow up in some exotic locations. Indonesia, and such. She'll be joining us later."

The clock on the mantelpiece struck three with a triple chime, reminding Rex of precious minutes ticking by before Patricia's guests arrived for the ceremony. It had been three days since Archie's alleged murder and in this heat he would decompose in a hurry. Had Patricia put him in the freezer? Reining in these disturbing thoughts, he asked Patricia who else could have had access to Archie's bowl.

"No one. I kept his bowl and water dish in the conservatory," she repeated herself, as old people tended to do. "That's where he could go in and out through his cat flap." She took a deep breath and appeared to draw strength from her inner core. "No one could get in there from outside. You can take a look."

"I shall, of course. I just want to get all the

facts first. The back garden is completely enclosed by the wall, but you can access it through a side gate."

"That's correct. In recent years, Archie did not attempt to jump over the wall. He was content to stay within the garden and just contemplate nature. Of course, when he was younger he loved to roam in the woods. I had many an anxious moment, I can tell you, when I thought he might have got lost or come to harm. But I felt it would have been cruel to keep him inside the house and restrict his natural instincts. It would have been tantamount to smothering someone's creative freedom, don't you think? And he did get into some fine adventures!" Patricia's pale blue eyes lit up behind her lenses. "All fodder for my little books. And he always came home before I became too sick with worry, bless his sweet heart."

"And you're sure no one could have come into the house without your knowledge?" After all, at her age she could have easily forgotten to lock a door.

"The kitchen door and front door are the only means of entry. I always lock myself in. And I never leave the downstairs windows open when I'm not in the room. It's always possible someone could come through the woods and climb over the wall and steal something."

Rex rather thought a thief would go into

shock when he saw the contents piled and crammed into the house, realizing he would have to root through everything to find something worthwhile. There were knickknacks and figurines galore, but they did not appear to his eye to be worth a great deal in resale value. Obviously, though, they held sentimental value for Patricia, else she would have thrown them out or donated them to a jumble sale; unless she was a compulsive hoarder.

At that moment the doorbell rang and Patricia responded immediately, cocking an ear, so she probably wasn't so very deaf, after all. "That'll be Dot," she said, getting up heavily with one hand on the armrest. "She said she'd come early to help with tea."

Rex heard voices in the hall, the deep one Patricia's, the other high-pitched, almost strident in its animation. "I brought a homemade ginger cake topped with toasted almonds," it said. "And some chocolate fingers from the shop."

"You are such a dear. Just set the cake down in the kitchen. Perhaps the biscuits should go in the refrigerator? Connie prepared some sandwiches. I don't know where she and Charles have got to. They went out for a walk after lunch. And Reginald Graves has arrived from Edinburgh. Come and meet him. He's the son of one of my dearest friends. I must have mentioned Moira to you."

A woman who looked to be in her late seventies entered the room with a cane. Rex leapt to his feet to greet her and found himself towering over her head of tight bluish-grey curls.

"I'm Dot Sharpe," she introduced herself before Patricia could. Rex tried not to notice that her nose aptly suited her surname. "Patricia's friend and a fellow writer," she crowed.

"Delighted. Rex Graves at your service." He held out his hand and took her tiny appendage into his paw.

"Dot, we are just finishing up some family chat before the others get here. We won't be much longer."

"Oh, of course. Well, I'll be in the kitchen. You carry on. We'll chat later, Rex," Dot said amiably. In spite of her walking stick, she took herself off in spry fashion, and Patricia closed the door after her.

"I don't want her to know I suspect murder," she confided, sitting back down.

"Is she one of the suspects?" Rex asked.

"Doubtful, but who knows? I've invited everyone I can think of who might have had a hand in Archie's death. Not that I necessarily think them capable, but because they had opportunity. Means, motive, and opportunity. Isn't that how it goes?"

"It's a good place to start. How many people are coming?"

25

"Well, Noel Cribben from next door."

"Whose dog Archie allegedly attacked. A motive, possibly?"

"We mended our fences, so to speak, as all good neighbours must. I gave him a signed collection of Claude books. For all I know, he sold it to pay the veterinary fees. Dr. Doug Strange may drop by. He thought Archie a fine fellow. He came on a couple of house calls. Nothing serious. Once when Archie had a bit of mange on his face and another time when he had the sniffles. Couldn't do anything for Archie this time. I put his food out at six as usual, before I went to my book club. I was back by eight or so. When he didn't come back in by nine, I got concerned. He always came upstairs to read with me in bed last thing at night. It was beginning to get dark so I took a torch and looked in the back garden. I found him lying in the flower bed with vomit nearby. I knew he was dead, but I called Strange all the same. You know, just in case."

Rex felt his eyes grow moist and discreetly wiped away an incipient tear. Patricia touched his hand.

"Thank you, Reginald. It's plain to see why your mother is so proud of you. You always were such a dear boy. And such a gifted pupil and student. You are a credit to Moira, indeed."

Rex was quite overcome. If he had managed not to succumb to tears before, he would have failed now had Patricia not suddenly distracted him by rummaging under the *sofa cushions. Finally she retrieved a note from beneath a knitting magazine. She handed it to him and waited expectantly. Rex unfolded the paper, which read, in block capitals, "*SAY GOODBYE TO ARCHIE,*" just as his mother had told him.

"Aye," he said. "Perhaps it's telling that it says Archie and not Claude."

"Exactly. That's what makes me think it's less likely to be a stranger."

"And the person took care not to reveal his or her handwriting by cutting out letters from a newspaper."

"And probably wore gloves so as not to leave fingerprints."

"Did it come in an envelope?"

"Yes, with just my first and last name typed on it and posted through my letterbox some time Wednesday afternoon. But I didn't know that at the time because Charles picked it up and put it on the hall table with all the junk mail, and I didn't find it until Thursday morning, when it was too late." Realizing she had raised her voice, Patricia put a hand to her mouth. Rex could hear crockery rattling in the kitchen down the hall, and then the sound of the front door opening, followed by voices.

"That'll be Charles and Connie." Patricia took the note from Rex's hand and hid it between the pages of the magazine.

"Was the envelope sealed?" Rex asked.

"No, it just had the flap tucked in."

"Have you shown this note to anyone?"

"No one. I wanted to speak to you first."

"Keep it hidden for now. Who else is coming this afternoon?" Rex glanced at the old-fashioned clock on the mantelpiece. It was a quarter to four.

"Roger Dalrymple, whom I mentioned when we were discussing my will. Rather a colourful character. I think you'll enjoy him."

"He lives in Woodley?"

"He does, and by some stroke of luck he became my illustrator. He's a painter, you know. Was in advertising before. Well, when I got my idea for Claude, I asked if he'd be interested in coming up with a few cat drawings for my stories. He took some photos of Archie, and I told him what sort of attributes my fictional cat possessed, and he came up positively trumps. We sold the series almost right away. And it took off!" Patricia looked amazed, even after all these years.

"So the series is a joint endeavour, and couldn't survive without either partner, I assume?"

"We're not equal partners. It's a sixty-forty split, which I think is fair. After all, the series was my idea. And it's made Roger quite famous. Before, he was just selling a few pictures at art fairs and to friends."

"What aboot merchandising. Have you explored that angle?"

"Oh, Reginald, you are so clever! My son suggested we did that years ago, but I didn't like the idea of Claude being paraded around on school bags and tee-shirts."

Archie would have been none the wiser, Rex thought; even when he was alive. "How does Roger feel aboot it?" he asked.

"He likes the idea of capitalizing on Claude, but can't do anything without my say-so. I deplore the notion that an artist would sink so low, but he was in advertising, so I suppose he must have sacrificed some scruples along the way. Anyway, it's a moot point now," she said with a hopeless shrug of the shoulders.

"Why so?"

"Because Archie is dead!" she cried out. "There is no more Claude."

Rex patted her hand. "I think I understand how you feel. But give it time. You may change your mind."

"I shan't. It's over. It would be too painful to sit at my computer trying to conjure up stories without Archie there on the desk giving me inspiration. He did, you know. It's as though he communicated them to me. Oh, I'm so lonely without him! I miss his chunnering and chirruping. Just seeing him laze in the sun or chase after a butterfly, jumping up with his paws in the air, made me joyful. He never caught one though. One time he swiped at a Swallowtail and took off the tip of its wing. I saved it and it managed to fly away. But I got a story out of that." Patricia expelled a shuddering breath. "My creative juices have dried up. There's not much left to live for."

Rex was quite used to the morbid ramblings of elderly people, essentially living with two at home, and let her comment pass. "Could someone ghost write your stories until you're ready to resume?" he suggested. "Perhaps someone who knew Archie?"

"But it wouldn't be authentic. I'm sure my readers would see right through it. Do you believe in ghosts, Reginald?"

"Ehm, there might be a strong spirit presence that exists in the form of energy, I suppose," he hedged. "Why do you ask?"

"It's Archie. He's been trying to tell me something. I have a premonition of my own death."

*

While Rex was contemplating this strange announcement, Dot poked her curly head around the door. "Sorry to disturb you. Shall we set the table beneath the oak? There's plenty of shade there."

"Are Charles and Connie lending a hand?" Patricia asked.

"Yes. Charles said to lay out the paisley cloth and the Spode tea service."

"That's fine."

"Felicity just got here. I told her you were busy catching up with an old friend." Dot gave Rex an ingratiating smile.

"I'll be along in a minute."

Dot nodded and shut the door after her.

"She means well," Patricia said. Clearly she found Dot a trifle irritating, as evidenced by the set of her jaw.

"Who is Felicity?" Rex asked, keeping a mental account of Patricia's acquaintance.

"My agent and publicist. She came down from London on Wednesday afternoon to discuss some business with me. And she's down again for Archie's send-off."

"That's nice of her. Archie's demise must be a blow to her."

"Of course. He was Claude, after all, and she did well out of him. Fifteen per cent of my earnings!"

"Did she do the publicity for a fee?"

"Yes. The publicist at my publishing firm doesn't do very much. Alder Press is only a small publisher." She gave a resigned sigh. "Well, I suppose we'd better join them. It's almost four."

The clock on the mantelpiece confirmed this a

minute later with a peal of chimes. Rex helped Patricia out of the sofa, but before they could make it to the door, a tall elderly gentleman sauntered into the room and introduced himself to Rex as Roger Dalrymple.

"Aye, pleased to meet you," Rex said. "My son enjoyed your illustrations growing up."

"Love the Scottish accent, old chum. Patricia's lost a bit of hers." Roger stooped slightly, but was in good shape for his age. He also had all his hair, white, and downy as plumage. He was dressed in a light cashmere cardigan, which he removed and draped carefully over a piece of furniture, as Rex had done with his jacket. Roger had likewise put on a black tie in keeping with the solemn occasion.

"We're taking tea outside." Patricia led them to the kitchen where Dot and Connie, whom Rex recognized as his hostess' middle-aged daughter, stood arranging items on a tray. Dot was looking down her pince-nez at a pile of teaspoons and small forks and counting them with nods of her head, while Connie stacked cups and saucers on the tray. Rex said hello and how nice it was to see her again. She gave a harassed smile and mumbled a greeting that trailed off mid-sentence as she continued fumbling with the crockery. A patchwork bag with a pair of needles sticking out of the opening sat on a kitchen chair.

"We're eight, is that right, Patricia?" Dot

asked, diminutive next to her friend.

"Yes. Where's Charles?"

"Setting out the table and chairs."

"Anything I can take?"

"Perhaps Rex could take the tray?"

"Be glad to," he said.

"Roger can take the cake."

"I always do!" he joked, nudging Rex's arm.

Patricia opened the kitchen door where a crazy-paving path continued around the house into an English cottage garden worthy of a picture postcard. A low wall of mellowed brick, matching that of the eighteenth century home, enclosed a border of flower beds surrounding a lush green lawn at whose centre stood an ornate bird bath carved in white stone. The word that came to Rex's mind was "charming."

"I put a bell on Archie's collar so he couldn't get at the birds," Patricia informed him as they made towards the table beneath the spreading oak tree. "They'd hear him coming and take off. He had more success with field mice, which he'd bring to the kitchen door before I had the conservatory put in." Jutting from the back of her cottage, the glass extension housed a couple of recliners and some exotic plants in large earthenware pots. A rubber cat flap in a bottom pane had enabled Archie to come and go as he pleased. "And he used to terrorize the squirrels in his younger days, but couldn't quite get up to the top of the trees."

On two sides of the garden stood a wood of birch and pine. To the right, looking out, Rex could see the neighbour's greenhouse and part of a two-storey home in the same brick. He asked Patricia where she had placed Archie's bowl, and she pointed to a tiled spot near a corner taken up by one of the plants.

"Beside the fern. I always kept it there."

The bowl, angled a couple of feet from the cat flap, would have been too far away for someone to reach in, spike the contents with poison, and then put the dish back in its place.

Charles was standing by the tea table apparently pondering the disposition of chairs. These were wicker and padded with cushion seats. So far they had been arranged in a loose circle beside the table, capitalizing on the shade provided by the oak tree. Rex set down the laden tray.

"Delighted you could come!" Charles, transpiring under a short-sleeved shirt clinging to his chubby frame, stuck out a hand. "How's your mother?"

"Quite well. But she has a phobia about travelling. She's becoming a bit of a recluse, I fear."

"So I heard. They get more petulant and childish with age, don't they?" Charles spoke in a conspiratorial tone, pointing his head in his mother's direction. Patricia stood on the lawn talking to a dainty man with a thatch of snowy hair and wearing a light linen suit and yellow bowtie. "The dandy yonder is the neighbour whose dog was mauled by Archie, leaving a disfiguring scar on his nose. Cutie Pie is a fluffy white poodle. Noel was going to enter him at Crufts, but can't show him now. Huge big row over it. The vet patched him up as best he could, but he's an animal doctor, not a plastic surgeon. All hopes dashed of him winning Best in Show. Noel and my mother are still feuding about it."

It looked like things were heating up between Noel and Patricia even as they spoke.

"I thought they'd buried the hatchet," Rex said.

"Hardly. She's still incensed about her delphiniums even though they've all grown back. It's so terribly petty!"

Rex glanced over to the length of wall dividing the two properties, where indigo, mauve, white, and pink spires swayed in the gentle breeze. Closer to the cottage, a profusion of purple foxglove enticed lazily buzzing bumble bees to their tubular flowers whose dark spots led to the nectar. In the gait of a younger man, Roger Dalrymple strolled toward the two men with his hands in his trouser pockets.

"What a heavenly day," he said looking up at the hazy blue sky flocked with white clouds.

Charles did not appear convinced. "I'll be glad when it's over and I can get back to London. Got a pile of work waiting for me at the office." He mopped his ruddy face with a paper napkin from the pocket of his shorts, which made him look all the more like an overgrown schoolboy. "I'll have to head back as soon as poor Archie's in the ground."

"So you're not staying the night?" Rex asked, glad Charles would not be required to sleep on the couch.

"No, but if you are, you're more than welcome to my room."

Rex thanked him. Charles nodded and ambled away in the direction of the house, leaving him alone with Roger.

"He can't stand being under his mother's roof for more than two days," the illustrator said, nodding after Charles. "I expect Connie and Charles are a disappointment to her. Neither did particularly well in school or achieved anything remarkable in life. Sometimes I think Patricia cared more about Archie than she did her own children."

Rex refrained from commenting, but he got the same impression. He could not remember who was the eldest, but each looked older than their years up close, even though Connie's pixie-cut dark hair streaked with plum strived for a young and carefree look.

"It's not just about the delphiniums, you know," Roger was saying as he watched Noel and Patricia talking more civilly to one another now, but maintaining a rigid stance. The poodle could be heard yapping in its garden. "You see, I'm friends with both Patricia and Noel, and they each expect me to take sides. So I'm caught in the middle. I have a working relationship with Patricia, which makes things awkward and puts a strain on my friendship with Noel."

"And it's a very small village," said Rex, suspecting that Roger enjoyed the drama and being at the centre of it.

"Exactly. And to be honest, I can't stand the dog. Cutie Pie!" Roger stuck two fingers in his throat and made a gagging motion. "At least Archie had some dignity. He didn't slobber and roll over on his back for just anyone."

"Tea, everyone," Patricia announced, lumbering towards them. "Making any headway," she asked Rex before he could follow Roger to the table.

"Just getting to know the characters in the plot, so to speak."

"I knew you'd suss it out. Yes, here we have the chief suspects assembled. Noel only came because he can't resist a free tea. Such a detestable little man. What they say about dogs and their owners is true. If Noel were a dog, he'd be a pretentions little poodle! Now come along," she

37

directed. "Dot bakes a delicious cake."

Rex followed her to the mouth-watering spread on the table. Connie brought out the tea tray loaded with plates of sandwiches covered in clinging film. She set it down and removed an envelope.

"Mum, the kids made you a card. They wanted to be here, of course, but as it's their weekend with their dad..."

Patricia opened the envelope with a sigh. "Children need stability," she opined. Inside was a homemade collage of a black cat clearly made by primary-schoolers. "Very thoughtful," she said. "Please thank Miranda and Matt." She set it aside and gazed at the tea table as though overwhelmed.

"Shall I be mother?" Dot immediately began dispensing tea while Connie, clearly disappointed by her mother's lukewarm reaction to the card, passed around plates of cucumber and watercress sandwiches.

"Archie so enjoyed his milk," Patricia said to no one in particular. "Some people claim it doesn't agree with cats, but Archie wasn't lactose intolerant."

Rex intercepted a glance of mild exasperation between Connie and Charles. He doubted their mother doted on her two grandchildren as much as she had her cat. She'd had her son and daughter late in life, a resigned spinster by the time she found love. Connie, too, had waited a long time to have children, and seemed exhausted by the process of motherhood. But perhaps it was the ex-spousal arrangements that were weighing her down. Whatever the situation, she and her brother regarded their mother with a measure of wariness. Connie now assumed a slightly bossy tone in her admonitions as Patricia started rearranging the chairs that Charles had set out on the lawn.

"Mother, you know you shouldn't be exerting yourself. Remember what Dr. Beaseley said."

"Everyone calls him Dr. Beastly," Roger said in an aside to Rex, having returned from the house with his cardigan. "The bedside manner of Hitler! I was evacuated during the war, you know. The children in our London borough were sent by train into the countryside during the blackout and bombings. I remember the sense of freedom and all the wonderful sights and smells. As soon as I retired from my advertising job in the City, I couldn't wait to move to the country. At times it still feels like I'm returning to my boyhood."

Roger certainly seemed young at heart, Rex mused. "I used to stay in Swanmere, not far from here."

"I go there sometimes to sketch the swans in the pond. So glad you could come down. I understand your mother was at school with Patricia."

"Aye, but she doesn't travel well, so I'm here

in loco."

They watched a woman stalking about the garden in heels that left dents in the grass. "Oh, how lovely," she enthused over the cut flower beds and forest of foxglove, flitting to and fro and extending her arm in an arc to throw out crumbs for the birds.

"A Londoner," Roger uttered with disparagement. "As once was I," he added in a more light-hearted tone. "Still, ruining the lawn with those stilettoes makes me wince."

"Who is she?"

"That's our literary agent. Felicity Parker & Associates is a boutique agency occupying premises in one of the less smart addresses in London, not that you'd know it to look at her." The trim, fiftyish woman in question wore what looked to be an expensive suit along with the high heels, both inappropriate for an informal garden party, in Rex's view. She sported a modern haircut where the back was bluntly cut shorter than the sides, of an unnatural hue that clashed with the puce silk blouse frilled around the cuffs and throat.

"Oh, right. Patricia mentioned her."

"She represents children's, soft-boiled mystery and cookery books. Drat it, I lost a button off my favourite cardie." Roger was looking down at the garment folded over his arm. "How did that happen?"

"Must have caught on something."

"I suppose. But I only just brought it out of the house, thinking I might get cold if the sun went in. I didn't notice the button was missing when I put it on earlier. Oh, well, I kept the spare it came with."

"Run home and fetch it," Dot said as if Roger were capable of running anywhere. She sat by the table blithely knitting away while she spoke. "I'll sew it on for you. It won't take but a jiffy."

"Oh, thank you, Dot. What would we do without you!" Roger patted down the pockets of his trousers, found his keys, and made for the side of the cottage, leaving the cardigan on the arm of a wicker chair beside Dot's.

From her patchwork bag she selected a small card wrapped with yarn. "This will match closely enough," she said holding it out to the cardigan whence dangled a thin wool strand. "They never secure the buttons properly." She drew out a pair of sewing scissors from the bag and cut off a length of yarn in readiness for Roger's return.

Rex helped himself to the delicate white triangles of watercress and cucumber sandwiches and a slice of the ginger cake, which was set on a plate covered with a paper doily. He took a chair beside Connie, who had heaped her plate full of food.

"Shall I be mother again?" Dot chirped from the table, standing over the tea pot decorated with roses. "There's some left in the pot."

The elderly woman was a dynamo, Rex reflected. It was as though she could not stand to be idle.

"Please do," Patricia replied. "Perhaps Connie can help serve." She looked pointedly at her daughter. The hapless woman set down her plate on her chair where the chocolate fingers soon began to melt in the heat.

Roger plopped onto a seat on Rex's other side holding a wedge of cake. "Found the spare button," he said, pleased. He looked around with a wry expression. "Jolly occasion, I must say. Have you ever attended a cat's burial?"

Rex conceded that he had not.

"Patricia's become a bit gaga, if you ask me. I'm surprised the editor didn't send her last two stories back for a rewrite. I was embarrassed to put my illustrations to them, truth be told. But then," Roger said with a winsome smile, "greed wins over pride!" He bit into the cake and gave a murmur of approval. "One can always rely on Dot to provide a good tea, even if she is an interfering old busy-body."

"I cannot really concur that Patricia has lost her marbles," Rex said. "She seems remarkably lucid to me. In fact, she appears to be holding it together rather well considering she lost Archie only three days ago."

"Funny you should say 'lost.' That's what I

mean, really. She's become forgetful. Well, age will do that to the best of us. But I'm not just talking about being able to hold a story together. She's been getting clueless about things. Leaving her purse in shops, forgetting to put the rubbish out on the right day. All that precedes Archie's death."

"Forgetting to lock her doors?" Rex asked.

"That sort of thing. Two weeks ago she forgot to tell me she'd made a change in the proofs for the latest book, which necessitated me making a modification to one of the illustrations. So now I had to show Claude with a canary in his mouth instead of a mouse. Thank goodness it wasn't the cover. Fortunately, someone in the editing department caught it before the book went to print and called me direct, but it was last-minute stress, and I have to watch the old blood pressure."

Rex did not think Roger looked like someone who needed to watch either his weight or his blood pressure. He appeared incredibly fit for his age.

"Just telling Rex about our little mouse-up with the publisher, Patricia," Roger said wickedly as the writer approached with a cup of tea.

"Yes, sorry about that mix-up over the mouse," she said, and sipped her tea. "You came up trumps. And the canary was so much more *Claude*, don't you think?"

"I do," Roger replied with too much enthusiasm. Connie returned and sat down dejectedly with her melted biscuits and stale wilted sandwiches.

"The level to which I have sunk," Roger resumed when Patricia was out of earshot, and yet not seeming to care if Connie heard. However, she seemed wrapped up in her own thoughts, and Rex returned his attention to the illustrator. "I used to be quite a successful painter, in the Impressionist style, actually."

"But you are better known for Claude," Connie replied to Rex's surprise. Apparently she had been paying attention, after all, if only the vaguest of sorts.

"This is true." Roger hung his head. "I should not sound so churlish and ungrateful. I just wish Patricia would do something with the Claude merchandizing rights. Felicity has failed to persuade her. By God, children should be walking around in Claude tee-shirts and with him on their satchels and gym bags."

"I think that's precisely what Patricia wants to avoid," Rex said.

"Why ever not, though? After all, Claude is educational. Did you know the meaning of contradictory when you were knee-high to a grasshopper?" Roger asked him.

"I did," Connie retorted. "And look where it got me."

44

"Oh, come off it, old girl. You're well rid of Nigel. He had absolutely no imagination. Running off with his secretary, indeed!"

"They're not called that anymore, Roger! And what does it matter? She's young and she's pretty, and I'm stuck with bringing up two kids on my own!" Connie burst out of her chair, knocking it backwards onto the grass and spilling her tea.

"Oh, dear," Roger said watching as she stumbled back to the house. "Did I say something wrong?"

"You probably should not have said anything at all. Seems she's still bit raw over her divorce."

"Nigel was a swine. Why does she persist in mooning over him?"

Rex was not there to answer that question and wished Roger had not caused Connie to leave. Or had he done so on purpose? Rex glanced at him innocently drinking his tea. Charles came hobbling towards them and took Connie's vacated chair.

"What's up with Connie?" he asked. "Rushed past me in tears. Did Mother upset her again?'

"No, it was me," Roger admitted. "I'm afraid I put my foot in my mouth. Say, what's wrong with your own foot?"

"I tripped over one of Archie's mice. The black-and-white chequered thing with cat nip in it that he liked so much. I think I sprained my ankle. Dot's fetching some ice. I don't know why

Mother doesn't get Faye in once a week to tidy up. It's not like she can't afford it, and Faye needs the money. The place is such a mess you can barely see the floor. Someone's going to have a really bad fall one of these days. Ouch," Charles exclaimed, stretching out his leg and depositing his sandaled foot gently on the soft bed of grass.

Dot approached on her cane with a bag of frozen peas and handed it to Charles with instructions to place it on his swollen ankle for twenty minutes.

"You are such a busy bee," Roger said. Rex could not tell if he was mocking her.

Charles thanked her profusely and bent forward to wrap the packet around his bare ankle.

"Would you like some more tea, Reginald?" Dot asked.

There was nothing Rex would have liked more, and said he would get it himself.

"Sit, sit," she told him before he could get up, holding out her arm for his cup and saucer. "Milk, sugar?"

"Aye. One, thank you."

"Note how she didn't ask if I wanted any tea," Roger said with amusement as she hobbled to the table.

"Well, she only has the one hand," Rex pointed out. A walking cane occupied her other.

"Wouldn't have made a difference. She doesn't like me."

"And why is that?"

"She's jealous of my relationship with Patricia. Dot is a wannabe writer. Doubt she's any good, but she's always pestering Patricia with questions about writing and gets resentful when I'm here at the house trying to get some actual work done."

This triangle involving Patricia reminded Rex of the one Roger had mentioned existed with Noel, the neighbour. It all seemed unnecessarily complicated and childish. "Well, Dot is sewing on your button," he reasoned.

Roger shrugged his narrow shoulders. "I tried attending her book club, but really, it was too pretentious. I felt outnumbered by all the women. This village is full of old biddies. If I weren't so attached to my cottage, I'd leave. It must be something in the sea air. They just keep on going on. They're indestructible."

"Noel doesn't attend the book club?"

"No, he's got more sense. As do the other men around here. They're probably glad to get rid of their wives of a Wednesday evening and watch whatever they want on the telly."

"Where is the book club held?"

"It's a revolving thing. The members take turns to host it. It's usually a wine and cheese do."

"Do you happen to know where it was held this past Wednesday?"

"When Archie took sick, you mean? Are you sleuthing?" Roger grinned, baring a fine set of teeth, which might have been false. "You're a Crown prosecutor up in Scotland, aren't you?"

"I am."

"It must be hard to switch off from asking questions, am I right?"

"Something like that," Rex prevaricated. Roger was a shrewd fellow, the sort of person you never knew quite where you stood with. Rex did not wish to divulge too much.

"It was held at Madeline's," Roger said. "She runs a small bed-and-breakfast to help pay her mortgage. Her husband ran off, just like Connie's, but made it all the way abroad. Took the lady of the manor with him. That white mini-mansion on the hill. She was the doctor's wife."

"Dr. Beaseley's?"

"Yes, but remember, we call him Beastly around here. And you know what's even stranger about Dr. Strange's name, the local vet's?"

Rex was not sure any of this was relevant to his cat murder inquiry, but asked the required question anyway.

"His middle name is Moore!" Roger laughed with childish delight. "As if Strange wasn't enough."

"Getting back to the Wednesday book club, you seem well-informed for someone who doesn't attend anymore."

"Well, they're always wittering on about it. I don't know what they'll do when they run out of

Jane Austen."

Dot came back with Rex's tea, apologizing for it having taken so long. "I had to make a fresh pot," she explained.

"Don't worry about me, Dot," Roger said pointedly. "I'll get my own." And rose to do so.

"Roger is a frightful gossip," she said to Rex. "I don't know what he's been telling you, but you should take everything he says with a grain of salt."

"He was just telling me aboot your book club. My mother enjoys hers." Rex explained it was one of the few things that got her out of the house.

"Shame she doesn't live here. We could do with some new blood." Dot sat down stiffly in Roger's chair, resting her cane against her knees, and slid the handles of the patchwork bag from her arm. Within seconds she was knitting again, needles jabbing and clicking.

"How many members do you have?" Rex asked casually, stirring his tea.

"Seven now. All women!"

"That's a good turnout for such a wee village." He wondered how he could ask which guests at the tea party had been present without seeming too obvious. "Does Connie attend when she's staying at her mother's?"

"No, she never has. And she didn't arrive until after…you know. But we do have a guest on occasion. This week it was Felicity Parker giving some tips on how to find an agent. She had some business with Patricia and was kind enough to stay for the club."

Rex looked around for Felicity.

"She's inside with her client," Dot informed him. "Fortunately, the story's almost finished. Patricia said she can't bear to look at it. Says it's her last one."

"Hopefully, Felicity will persuade her otherwise."

"I think she's in there doing just that."

Roger, returning with his refill of tea and a glass of lemonade, said Patricia probably just wanted to get on with burying her cat and for everyone to go home. He drew up a spare chair, since Dot was sitting in his.

"Roger," she said in a whining voice, "I sometimes think you say things just for effect, without the least regard for how they might sound."

"Just as well I'm not a writer then. I'd be censored right, left and centre by every book club in Britain!"

"Roger's right," Charles interjected from his chair, removing the peas from his ankle. "Once Archie is laid to rest, perhaps we can all get back to our lives."

*

"Charles, don't be so heartless," Dot said.

"I didn't mean to be."

"What are you knitting, Dot?" Roger asked. "Is that robin egg blue? Lovely colour."

"It's a baby blanket for the WI."

Rex was hypnotized by Dot's deft fingers as the woollen square grew before his eyes.

"Archie was ailing, let's not forget." Roger set his empty cup under his chair. "Better to have him go out with a bang. I'm sure Felicity will put out a press release. There'll be a surge in sales once word gets out. Perhaps news of his 'murder' will introduce Claude to a whole new readership. 'Who is the cat killer?' everyone will be asking. Can you imagine the outrage from cat lovers all over the world?"

"You don't sound overly fond of Archie," Charles remarked. "For one who created his fictional image."

"He was a cat, for God's sake. Naturally, I'm sorry for Patricia. I know it's hard to lose a pet, especially a cash cow. But Archie was not the saint she makes him out to be. He got to be very demanding, imperious even, and she was at his constant beck and call. Archie this, and Archie that. And would you just look at Archie!" Roger downed the rest of his lemonade and crunched on an ice cube. Rex wondered again if he wore dentures. He was still a handsome man, if a bit haughty-looking.

"Not to mention the hairballs he chucked up all over the place," Charles said with distaste. "One time I found one on the bed."

Rex wished now he'd been more insistent about staying at Madeline's bed-and-breakfast.

"Truth be told," said Roger, who seemed inclined to tell the truth at every turn, "the last two Claude books didn't do nearly as well as their predecessors, like I told Rex earlier. It appears the great Patricia Forsyth is losing her touch and running out of ideas."

"Really, Roger!" Dot chided without missing a beat in her sewing.

He continued regardless. "Sales have dwindled dramatically, according to her editor, whom I dined with last week. *Claude the Contortionist Cat* and *Claude the Contrary Cat* had 'weak and predictable plots,' the reviews said, and lacked the cautionary aspect that parents had come to love so much. 'See what happened to Claude when he got too inquisitive?' " Roger said, his voice denoting quotation marks. " 'That's right! His tail got stuck in a mousetrap!' Or, 'Look what happened to Claude when he gazed in the mirror once too often. He saw the image of a bigger, meaner cat that Horrible Harry had pasted over the looking glass, and was so frightened he wouldn't look at his reflection again!' That was in *Claude the Conceited Cat.*"

"My son loved those books when he was a

bairn," Rex reminisced aloud. "Not sure it cured him of mirrors, though. He is pretty vain."

Roger barked out a laugh. "Aren't we all! Well, Archie's nine lives are well and truly over now, poor bugger. But at least his were blessed. And he made it to one hundred and twenty-six in human years! That I should be so lucky. Thank God it's a closed casket. Frankly, I find the whole thing frightfully gruesome. So much more pleasant if we could all be playing croquet on the lawn. Oh, there's Noel sitting on his own. Excuse me while I go say hello. I don't want him to think I'm avoiding him."

He wandered off, to Rex's disappointment. Roger had a penchant for gossip, which might come in useful. And he appeared to be perceptive. Perhaps with his artist's eye he could see behind the subject at hand. Certainly, Rex would not have wanted to be on the receiving end of his acerbic wit.

"This is Faye," Patricia announced out of the blue, practically dragging a young woman over to Rex's chair. A rather delicate name for such a chunk of girl, Rex thought. Her appearance was slovenly, her dun hair loosely bound in a ponytail, her frock a size too big on her large frame.

"I 'do' for Mrs. Forsythe," she explained in a broad Sussex accent. Her slightly crossed eyes made her look slow-witted or else sly. "I didn't miss it, did I?" she asked her employer. "I wouldn't want to miss poor Archie's burial, only me mum needed me. I've so many younger brothers and sisters, you wouldn't believe!" she told Rex, who smiled at her candour. "I almost missed the bus."

"You're just in time," Patricia assured her.

Rex recalled that in the event of the cat surviving Patricia, the will provided that Faye should live at the Poplars and take care of him until his natural death, whereupon she was to receive a sizeable amount of money to start again somewhere, and the house would then go to Connie and Charles. In the reverse event, Faye would receive a gratuity of three thousand pounds, a substantial amount for a girl of her means.

Patricia moved off, muttering something about making sure everything was in place for the ceremony. Rex inferred he was meant to speak to the girl and find out what he could.

"This is very hard on her," she said, gazing after Patricia. "She was bonkers about Archie. He was the perfect nap cat-lap cat. Just a big softie, really."

"Hard on you too, she told me." Aside from being saddened by Archie's death, Faye must be disappointed not to benefit from the more generous terms of the will. But perhaps she was fonder of Patricia than Archie...

Faye plopped down on Roger's chair. Dot had

finished sewing his button on his cardigan and went to present it to him. Charles was limping around the tea table, so no one was within earshot as Rex prepared to glean what information he could from Patricia's fortnightly help.

"I understand that Patricia holds you in such high regard that she entrusted you with the care of her cat and also the house in the event of her demise."

Faye nodded solemnly. "I would've stayed here fulltime to take care of the place and Archie, if it had been the other way round than what happened, and been more than glad to do it. But I never really expected Archie to outlive Mrs. F. I mean, he was a cat. He was getting on in years, and she's as fit as a fiddle. It was just in case she was run over by a bus or something, I s'ppose. She couldn't bear the idea of him being homeless, and she didn't want him put with a family that might mistreat him, or him put back in a cat shelter. He didn't really like other cats."

"Or dogs," Dot remarked, returning to resume her knitting.

"What aboot Connie or Charles?" Rex asked Faye over the clatter of needles. "Couldn't they have taken care of him?"

"Miss Connie is too busy with her kids. And Mr. Charles has got only a small flat in London. Archie would've been miserable there. I think Miss Connie would like to live at the Poplars.

Without her mum, I mean. It's great for kids here. Nice and safe."

"Do you know if she left you something in her will in the current situation?" Rex enquired disingenuously, knowing the answer and taking the opportunity of Dot being in conversation with a new arrival standing over her chair, a man in Wellington boots who had a loud blustering voice.

"I'm sure I don't." The young woman blushed all over her plain face, though made significantly less plain by comparison with all the older guests. "I'm only part-time, but I been coming here going on four years."

So she would know the family quite well, Rex deduced from that. "If Connie or Charles could not have taken Archie in, could one of them not have moved back here?"

Faye's crossed eyes widened as she appeared to wonder at all his questions. But not for long. "Like I said, Miss Connie's got enough on her plate already what with being a single mum, and Archie did demand quite a bit of attention. And Mr. Charles isn't partial to cats. Mrs. F. wanted to keep Archie in his 'accustomed habitat,' is what she said, and," here Faye flushed again, "she confided to me that she didn't want Miss Connie's two kids what she called 'terrorizing' poor Archie."

Patricia interrupted to introduce the large man in wellies, who was holding, somewhat incongruously, a delicate china tea cup and saucer. "Reginald, I'd like you to meet Doug Strange. He's the local veterinarian. He can't stay long." She seemed anxious for him to talk to the vet, and took herself off again, leading Faye away with her on the pretext of needing her help.

"I dropped by to see how Patricia was getting on," the vet told Rex. He had a neatly clipped greying moustache that ran along the length of his top lip and put Rex in mind of a broom brush. "I was delivering a calf at the Parridge farm. I understand she plans a small ceremony here in the garden with a marble plaque to mark the spot. 'In loving memory of Archie,' sort of thing. 'May the wicked be avenged.' That bit is probably not part of the engraving, but I'm sure it's implied." Dr. Strange winked with complicity. "She's on a crusade to find out who killed her cat, as you know. Though she told everybody he had simply eaten some foxglove."

"I'm not sure of the details of the ceremony. But, aye, Patricia got me down here to look into Archie's possible murder."

"Presumably she thought you, being a barrister, could get to the bottom of it?"

"Something like that." No point going into his hobby of solving murder cases, which he undertook in his spare time. These had never involved an animal before. "She told me Archie had been poisoned."

The vet nodded. "Toxicosis. I found digitalis in his stomach. Patricia insisted I look for poison, having found some bits of purple petal in his vomit. Given the symptoms and evidence, I was able to narrow it down. Shame. Nice animal and a good patient. Didn't try to claw me up like a lot of cats when I examined him in the past. He seemed to understand it was for his own good."

"Would he have had many good years left?"

"Hard to say. Cats are among the most resilient of creatures, and very stoic. Sometimes it's hard to know how much they're suffering. Archie was slowing down, like the rest of us, but he still had quality of life. He was very alert, and, of course, brought Patricia so much comfort in her old age."

"No question about the poison, then?"

"None."

"Could he have eaten it accidentally?"

"Cats have more sense. Dogs, on the other hand, get into all sorts of things. In any case, I found the foxglove diced up in the contents of his stomach. Couldn't have done that himself. Stitched him back together, though, good as new. Patricia insisted."

"Have you come across other cases of pet poisonings?"

Dr. Strange pondered the question briefly, tea cup and saucer split between two strong hands. "Not deliberate, no." He looked Rex direct in the eye. "I hope you find out who did this, for Patricia's sake. And everyone else's."

*

Rex sat back in his chair as Dr. Strange moved off to talk to Noel. The little man in the yellow bowtie wore thick lenses in his glasses and appeared nimble and shrewd. Rex wanted to have a word with him as well, to try to determine how much rancour actually existed over the incident of his dog's nose. He wondered how much money Patricia's neighbour had stood to gain had Cutie Pie won an award at Crufts, though it probably wasn't all about the money, but also about prestige. Rex couldn't imagine owning a show animal. In as far as he had ever envisioned having a dog, it was a large shaggy affair bounding about his weekend lodge in the Highlands, not prancing around an arena before a panel of judges.

The only other person he had not had an opportunity to speak with was Felicity Parker. The literary agent had just reappeared around the side of the house looking somewhat exasperated. This might be a good moment. She might be in the mood to vent, and people who vented tended to leave discretion to the wind. He rose from his chair holding his tea cup and approached the table at the same moment as she did.

"Barely enough left in the pot for two," he

said, lifting it. "But by the looks of it, your need is greater. May I pour you a cup?"

Felicity glanced at him and her gaze fixed. She smiled, he thought, flirtatiously. She was not wearing a wedding ring.

"Oh, thank you, yes. I've just had a taxing half hour with Patricia. Not the easiest client," she added, looking at him for a reaction, perhaps gauging whether it was safe to engage him in her confidence. She fluttered scoops of black lashes above her pink blush and vermilion lip gloss. Altogether too much artifice for a face of her years, decided Rex, who preferred natural.

"Old people can be difficult," he commiserated, pouring out tea. "She's my mother's age. They were at school together. My mother is too frail to travel from Edinburgh, so I came on her behalf to offer our condolences to Patricia."

"You knew Archie?"

"Well, I met him many years ago. And got frequent news bulletins from my mother as to how he was getting on. Patricia sent me some of her early books for my son." He handed the agent her cup of tea and refilled his own with what was left.

"Oh." Felicity sounded disappointed. "I, uh, so you're married?"

"Widowed."

"Oh, I'm so sorry!" she said with too much

feeling.

"I've been a widower for a long time. And my son's all grown up. But he did enjoy the Claude books. He found the cat very endearing. Roger does a grand job with the illustrations. Really brings him alive. Well, I suppose Claude will live on in spite of what's happened." He looked at Felicity, waiting for an answer.

"Don't know about that. The last two books haven't earned back their advances, at least not yet. The Claude series is running out of steam. Roger didn't want to be associated with those last stories. 'Not up to snuff,' he said."

Rex could well imagine him saying that.

"The trade reviews lacked their usual hypey exuberance," Felicity went on. "Some online reviews were even making jokes like, 'What's next?: *Claude the Arthritic Cat? Claude the Geriatric Cat?* It was humiliating."

For Patricia or for you? Rex wondered.

"I've just been suggesting revisions for the latest manuscript in an attempt to save it, but Patricia is refusing to listen. Says her heart's not in it. And yet the deadline is coming up. She's really left it to the last minute this time."

"Could you not just take over?"

"I could. I'm a published author myself, and I know Claude inside out. I could probably swing it." Felicity looked pretty determined, but Rex knew Patricia was not one to be pushed around by anybody.

Charles came over and told them it was time to assemble at the burial site, and then left again.

"I'm so sad I never had a chance to say goodbye to Archie in person," Felicity said.

"That's the problem with sudden death. We always think of things we should have said and done." Rex grabbed her elbow as Charles almost bumped into her on his bum ankle on his way back from corralling the people in the wicker chairs.

"Well, let's get on with the show," Roger said joining the group following Patricia to the far side of the garden. "Enough of morbidly sitting around over tea and cake remembering poor old Archie. Isn't it all a bit back to front? Shouldn't we have buried him first?"

At the back by the woods, a grave large enough to accommodate the cedar casket lying beside it had been dug in readiness. Charles stood at one end of the casket and Roger at the other. In unison they bent to grip a brass handle each and with great care and ceremony laid Archie to rest in the earth amid the chaste white azaleas. Patricia had donned green gardening gloves and emptied a spade-full of earth onto the smooth wood surface. "Ashes to ashes, dust to dust," she murmured.

Charles took over depositing dirt until the casket was covered and about level with the flower bed. He then placed a commemorative black marble plaque on the ground engraved in gold with the words, *"Here lies Archie, beloved cat and muse."* Rex thought the word muse only needed an "o" to change it to mouse, and wondered if it had been done on purpose as a joke. He decided not, since Patricia wasn't the joking sort. Everyone stood about with their heads bowed in a moment of silence. Someone blew their nose. A female sobbed. Looking up, Rex saw that the sob had come from Faye, whose eyes were streaming. Connie, too, shed a tear.

"Dear Archie," Patricia addressed the burial spot. "You kept me company at my computer and reminded me of mealtimes when I got carried away. Cats have clocks in their brains," she informed the group of mourners. "Oh, Archie, I don't know what I'm going to do without you!" she cried out in anguish.

"There, there, old girl," Roger comforted her. "He's in a better place."

She scowled at him. Dot proceeded to recite Psalm 23, Patricia glancing up sharply when she said, "I will fear no evil." Rex felt a tremor of evil around him in that moment. Charles busily mopped his brow. Roger gazed serenely at the mound of newly turned earth. Its warm, fecund smell drifted on the breeze. At the end of Dot's recitation, Dr. Strange proffered a gruff amen. Rex and the other guests respectfully left Patricia to say her goodbyes in peace, and drifted back to the table and lawn chairs, while a few people wandered towards the side of the house. Patricia, relatively composed throughout the proceedings suddenly went berserk.

*

Rex, aware of a commotion behind him, a shift in the air, turned around when he heard the guttural yell, which resembled a war cry. Patricia wielded the spade before her like a battle axe and dove into the mass of foxglove by the wall dividing her property from Noel's, thrashing at the blooms and raking the tall stalks out of the ground. The purple and pink flowers were felled without mercy.

Charles fretted beside Rex. "She's being irrational. She might hurt herself." And yet he hesitated to go to his mother's side.

"Might be good therapy weeding out what killed Archie," Felicity said. "They would only serve as a horrible reminder." The agent had left a trail of heel prints embedded in the grass, Rex saw, looking back the way they had come.

"If she didn't want to be reminded, she wouldn't have photos of him all over the house," Charles retorted. Rex realized in that moment that he had seen no pictures of Charles or his sister.

Patricia bent stiffly over the spade, panting hard, her wrath, or at least her energy, seemingly spent. Rex rushed over to help her, as Charles followed. Before he could reach her, she stooped lower, pushing the spade aside, and picked something up. Straightening with difficulty she stood among the floral carnage looking at whatever it was.

"Patricia, are you all right?" The old lady's breath was still laboured. Rex placed a hand under her arm to support her.

Her fingers uncurled to reveal a round mother-of-pearl object. "I found a button." Her voice held a puzzled tone. "It looks like one off Roger's cardigan. What's it doing here?" she demanded, more to herself than Rex, it appeared. After all, how could he be expected to know the answer to that? "Roger has never shown an interest in the garden. Mostly we're inside working. Did you see him by the foxglove this afternoon?"

Rex told her he hadn't, though he had been outside for the duration of the tea party. She closed her hand around the button. "Don't say anything about this yet," she said, slipping it into her tweed jacket pocket. "Nor you, Charles," she added upon seeing her son. A new sense of purpose seemed to grip her. Her features hardened as she strode toward the tea table.

"I know that look," Charles said. "Someone's for it."

"Roger, most likely."

However, Patricia did not approach Roger. She held her hand out to the teapot as though checking to see if it was still warm. She then addressed her daughter, who nodded and grabbed it and made for the house.

"What is Mother up to, I wonder?" Charles, whose face reminded Rex of a worried cocker spaniel's, limped on his sore ankle towards the table.

Rex stayed by the destroyed bed of foxglove and calculated the distance from the cottage to be about twenty-five feet, which was approximately halfway to the back wall, beyond which stood the wood. He heard Noel excuse himself to Patricia. He needed to get home and put on the sprinklers, he said, as it hadn't rained since Wednesday and he had laid some new sod. Rex would not get an opportunity to talk to him, after all. Doug Strange was leaving too. As Rex approached the remaining guests, Felicity was saying goodbye to Patricia. She asked if he needed a lift back to London.

"Reginald is staying overnight," Patricia told her.

Rex thought Felicity looked disappointed, or perhaps he was imagining it.

"Oh. Well, goodbye," she said, holding out her hand, which he shook warmly.

Teetering on her high heels, to which clung clods of earth and grass, she made her way down the path to the gate, whipping out a packet of cigarettes from her handbag as she went.

"I should leave too," Charles said, looking enviously after her.

"You'll at least stay for supper," Patricia told him. "Dot brought a lamb stew. I don't think I can eat, but you and Connie dine with Reginald. I'll go and lie down for a spell." She instructed Connie to wake her in an hour and thanked Dot for the casserole without inviting her to stay to share it.

Roger loitered on the lawn, toeing the grass with his fine leather shoe. "Patricia," he said. "Let me know if there's anything at all I can do…"

But she didn't stop to listen and took off wearily towards the house. Roger helped Connie bring in the tea things, and Rex assisted Charles with the folding table and wicker chairs, which they carried into the large shed on the far side of the garden.

"I feel such a horrible sense of emptiness," Charles confided as he shut the shed door. "I keep thinking I'll turn around and there'll be. Never thought I'd miss Archie. I'm more of a dog person, not that I ever had a dog."

"The place will probably seem empty for a while," Rex agreed.

He spotted Noel in his garden and excused himself to Charles.

"We never got a chance to meet," he called

out conversationally over the low brick wall as a sprinkler on the neighbour's viridescent lawn started spraying water in a wide circle. A small white poodle, its size disproportionate to the volume of its bark, darted out from behind the greenhouse and began attacking the water. The dog could not have been larger than Archie. Probably a match in a fight, Rex thought. From this distance, he could not see the disfigurement on its pink nose.

"Save me having to give him a bath," Noel said, thumbing back at the wet poodle.

"Nice wee doggie," Rex felt obliged to say even as the barks penetrated his skull like tiny ice picks. "Listen, Mr. Cribben, I wanted to ask you if, by any chance, you saw anything suspicious Wednesday night this side of the wall."

"Funny you should ask. You're looking into Archie's 'murder'? Someone mentioned you were a barrister friend of Patricia's. Advocate, isn't it, in Scotland?"

"Correct."

"Yes, well, Dr. Strange appears convinced the cat was poisoned on purpose."

"And what do you think?"

Noel shrugged. "I think Patricia is hallucinating, and Doug Strange is just humouring her. It's much easier agreeing with her, as I've learnt to my cost."

"Still, the evidence—"

"The evidence!" Noel scoffed. "She's got you bamboozled, and all."

"If the vet is to be believed, and I don't really see why not, diced foxglove was found in the contents of Archie's stomach. I don't think a professional like Dr. Strange would say or agree that the cat was murdered if he wasn't."

Noel pondered this for a moment. "How do you know they haven't hatched this plot so they can blame me? This afternoon at tea Patricia practically accused me outright of being involved. That's what our little argy-bargy was about. I firmly believe she got everyone there so she could point the finger at me in public. I should never have gone." The neighbour's furious countenance turned a shade of crimson in the fading sun.

Rex would have preferred not to have been having this conversation over the garden wall, but he couldn't get any closer without stepping into the flower beds. Charles was over by the foxglove digging out what was left of the flowers and smoothing over the earth, making it more presentable.

"You asked if I saw something suspicious Wednesday night," Noel said. "Well, I may have. Couldn't swear to it, because I wasn't wearing my glasses at the time and it was getting dark."

"Go on," Rex encouraged him.

"Well, Patricia's house was dark so she must have gone out, presumably to her book club. I saw a figure in black approach via the woods back there and creep over her wall and then disappear. I was in the process of closing the upstairs curtains when I caught a glimpse. At first I thought it might be a burglar, but the intruder left within five minutes, returning the way he'd come."

"You said 'he'?"

"Well, it was dark, and I was getting ready for bed and not wearing my glasses, like I said. If I'd been sure I would have called the police. But we've never had any trouble in the village. Sometimes we get teenagers hanging out in the woods. Cutie Pie must've scared him off," his owner said proudly.

At the sound of his name, the poodle barked even louder and rolled his wet body in the grass.

"He'll need a bath now," Rex noted.

Noel nodded assent and shrugged. "I need to get the other sprinkler on," he said. "Unless there's anything else I can help you with?"

"No, but thank you." Rex gave a friendly wave and wandered back to the house, where he found Patricia in the downstairs study seated at her desk staring at a framed photo of Archie.

Rex was amazed to see that order reigned in the room, all the papers and files methodically organised on desks and shelves. A whole wall was dedicated to books; a step ladder standing nearby. The desk at which Patricia sat held a personal computer attached to a slim printer.

"I thought you were taking a nap," he said.

"It's not the same napping without Archie. I miss him so much!" Her gaze returned to the photograph of the cat reclining in a semi-circle. "He was left at the shelter because black cats aren't popular. That's what they told me. Some people are superstitious. A black cat crossing one's path is supposed to be unlucky. But Archie brought me nothing but joy and good fortune. All the other kittens had gone to homes." She smiled wistfully. "His ebony fur was soft as velvet and he was so friendly. As soon as I brought him home he lay on the Persian rug in the parlour and started purring. He followed me everywhere. And someone took all that away from me!" She bent almost double over the desk. Tears splashed onto her gnarled hands. She removed her glasses and blotted her eyes with the cuff of her tweed jacket. "I'm sorry," she said, pulling herself together. "I'm making a spectacle of myself."

Rex swiped at a tear of his own and sniffed back the rest. Sitting in a chair beside hers, he took one of her wet hands and pressed it in his. "We'll find oot who did this," he promised foolishly in fervid indignation. After all, he was not much closer to solving the case than when he first arrived, unless Noel's account could be believed.

When Patricia had sufficiently recovered, he

asked her about the premonition she had mentioned before tea.

"I have a recurring vision where I'm murdered with a letter opener or some other sharp object. It's been going on since Archie was taken. I believe he's trying to tell me something, just like when he communicated stories to me. I'd be writing them down at the computer while he contentedly cleaned his ears, knowing how clever he was." Patricia reached into her desk drawer and pulled out a wooden-handled ink blotter of the sort that rocked back and forth, and such as Rex had not seen in a long while. She must still write with ink, he realized. Very old-school.

"I found this yesterday morning with a red splodge on it." She held the instrument up so he could see the glaring crimson mark that had blossomed on the fresh blotting paper. "It wasn't there Thursday night."

"The splodge?"

Patricia nodded. "The blotter was out on the desk where it always was. I put it away afterwards."

Could it be blood? Rex wondered. Another warning, like the note? "Do you use red ink?"

"I do not. I have no red ink. I sign my books with green ink, using a quill."

"I always admired your signature," Rex said. The capital "F" of her last name was composed of a dramatic flourish, the ensuing letters elegantly scrolled.

"It's become something of a trademark, so I always take my quill and green ink when I do book signings. Only Roger and Felicity come into my office and Faye, of course, if I'm not working. But there's no lock on the door."

"Who was here between Thursday night and Friday morning?"

"People were in and out of the house all day to offer their sympathies. Connie was already here and Charles arrived in the early evening. I was in my study until ten at night. Nothing was amiss that I remember. I first noticed the red on the blotter at eight the following morning. Archie's definitely trying to tell me something. I've been racking my brains. A red blot. Dot. A button? I got my spare key back from Dot. She was quite offended, I think. And Roger's button in the foxglove patch is suspicious, to say the least."

"Pity Archie couldn't just write the letters and give us more of a clue."

Patricia looked at him as though disappointed in a bright pupil. "Well, he can't write, naturally."

Rex noted the present tense. Clearly Archie lived on in her mind.

"Sewing scissors." Patricia paused long enough to make Rex ask her what she meant. "Dot had a pair with her yesterday in her knitting bag. I saw them when she cut a length of yarn in the garden. You were sitting out there. You might have seen them. Before that, the bag was in the kitchen, on one of the chairs, and Roger's cardigan was in the back parlour were he left it."

"You're suggesting someone used the scissors to snip off his button?"

"Or else Roger lost it when he was getting the foxglove Wednesday night to poison Archie's food with."

"But would Roger wear his favourite cardigan to rummage in the garden?"

"Roger is not gifted with the greatest good sense," Patricia remarked. "But I'm convinced the red on the blotter points to either Roger or Dot." She sat back wearily in her leather chair. "Or could it be blood? It's all rather sinister, especially in light of the note."

"That's what I was thinking," Rex admitted. "But I didn't want to alarm you."

The old lady sighed dispiritedly. "Please tell Connie I won't be having dinner. I'm not hungry. I'll just stay here awhile."

"Can I bring you anything? Some tea, perhaps?"

"No, thank you, Reginald. I just need a bit of peace and quiet. It's been rather a tiring day."

"Patricia," he asked on his way to the door. "Do you have a paper knife?"

"Just this," she said, pulling out a wooden envelope opener with a handle carved in the shape of a thistle. "It was a present from your mother." She gave a wan smile.

Rex felt a small measure of relief. It did not look at all deadly.

*

Dinner promised to be a sombre affair. Clearly Charles was only staying out of politeness, and he had made it clear he needed to leave immediately afterwards to get back to London. Connie heated up the casserole and set the table in the kitchen, "Since it's just the three of us," she said. She extracted a batch of rolls from the microwave. The fluorescent lighting accentuated her crow's feet, the tramlines between her brows, and the brackets around her mouth. Charles opened a bottle of claret and after the first glass became more animated. After the second, his already ruddy cheeks were well flushed. Inevitably the conversation turned to Archie's death, and brother and sister talked in hushed tones even though Patricia had gone upstairs to bed.

"She would have left him the house. And a cat charity gets most of the money," Charles divulged, his tongue loosened by wine.

"You don't know that for sure," Connie said, ladling out seconds of stew to which Dot had added potatoes and carrots from her garden.

"As a matter of fact, I do," Charles revealed. "I saw the will."

"You never!" Connie exclaimed. "When?"

"Thursday night when I was… Well, never mind what I was doing. Mother's desk was unlocked and curiosity got the better of me. I got a paper cut for my trouble." He showed his sister a pale scar on his index finger. Rex had to wonder if the man was accident prone. A cut, and then a twisted ankle. "I've always wanted to know what was in that wretched will," Charles said. "And now I do."

Rex remained quiet during this exchange. In the siblings' excitement he was all but forgotten, although Connie gave him a guilty glance before eagerly asking her brother, "Well?"

Charles cleared his throat and leaned in conspiratorially. "Thanks to Archie popping off first, the terms of the will are more in line with what one might expect, though not enough to make either of us rich. Excuse us," Charles apologized to Rex. "You must think us very indelicate to be discussing private matters in front of a non-family member. But Connie and I don't get much of a chance to talk except on the phone. And Archie's death, murder, what have you, made me wonder about my mother's will. I knew she'd made some outrageous provisions in it in the event she went first. She was always talking to Archie about it. 'Don't you worry, Archie, you'll be well taken care of. You'll never have to go back to that horrible shelter!' " he mimicked in his mother's lowland Scots voice.

"Still," Connie hurriedly added for Rex's benefit, "We were shocked by Archie's murder. It was murder, Charlie," she insisted. "Dr. Strange wouldn't lie about a thing like that."

Rex read in Charles' expression a measure of relief that someone had bumped Archie off and released the property to the children. Charles gulped down the last of his wine and regarded the empty bottle with an air of regret. Florid of complexion, pouchy-eyed and jowly, he exhibited the signs of an habitual drinker.

"Who do you think killed Archie?" Rex said, setting his knife and fork in his empty plate.

"No one we know," Connie replied. "No one was in the house Wednesday evening when Mother was at the book club. Dot, who's the only other person apart from us who has a key, as far as I know, was at the book club too. And we weren't here, were we, Charlie? I arrived later."

"I was in London," her brother alibied.

"Your mother said you were here on Wednesday afternoon, though," Rex contradicted. Patricia had told him it was Charles who had picked up the anonymous note posted through the front door.

"In the afternoon, yes. But it was a lightening visit. There was a matter I wanted to discuss with Mother, but she was busy with Felicity."

"What matter?" Connie asked.

"I needed a small loan, if you must know. Anyway," Charles told Rex, "I didn't hear about Archie's death until Thursday morning."

"Mother said she tried to reach you on your mobile and on your landline."

"I didn't get her messages until Thursday morning. And even then, all she said was, 'Charles, call me back. It's urgent.' "

"I drove over straightaway," Connie told Rex. "Mother was beside herself. Dr. Strange had just left with Archie to perform a post mortem at her insistence."

Rex worried about Patricia's state of mind. Aside from her loss, she was under a lot of strain and pressure, not least of which was her looming deadline. "Does she often go to bed this early?" he asked.

"She said she was too upset to eat," Connie said. "I took her up some warm milk. She's beginning to look a bit gaunt, don't you think, Charlie? But she often goes to bed early to read," she told Rex. "And gets up at the crack of dawn."

*

Rex did the same and next morning found Patricia making tea. She appeared more composed and said she'd managed to sleep out of sheer exhaustion. She prepared hot buttered crumpets and placed a glass dish filled with homemade strawberry jam on the table.

"From Dot's garden," she informed him.

Rex tasted the jam, which burst with summer flavour. "It's excellent. Seems Dot has a green thumb. The stew was delicious, incidentally. Connie left you some for your lunch."

Patricia joined him at the kitchen table with a pot of tea. "Dot is very good at the domestic stuff. Now, tell me: Did you find out anything useful over dinner?"

"Well, for one thing, Charles received a paper cut in your study. Possibly he used the blotting paper to absorb the blood on his finger."

Patricia added sugar to her tea. "I see. No doubt he was snooping about hoping to find my will and see what I've left him. He's in dire financial straits, you know."

"Be that as it may, the blot was likely not a sign or an omen. You must push all such notions from your mind, Patricia. Especially since I think I may know who our culprit is." He had tossed and turned in Charles' single bed that night brainstorming. Patricia stiffened in her chair. "And once that person is exposed," he continued, "they will not dare harm you, if indeed that is their intention."

"You really have a clue who poisoned Archie?"

"I do. A few clues."

"Well, who on earth is it?" she demanded in

agitation.

First Rex proceeded to tell her about the darkly clad figure Noel thought he had seen on Wednesday night, but added that her neighbour might be making up the story to avoid personal blame. Or perhaps it had been Patricia he had seen looking for her cat. Noel had said it was getting dark, and Archie would have already been dead, according to the vet, whom she had called after nine when she found him in the flower bed.

"Or else Noel is making up the story because it was him," Patricia declared. "I was not dressed in particularly dark clothes. But he couldn't have been in the house Wednesday evening. In fact, today was the first time since the injury to his dog's nose that he's been round here. How could he have tampered with Archie's food?"

"By using a gardening implement or other tool to hook the bowl?"

"Yes, of course! How silly of me not to have thought of that. No one had to be in the house, did they? The bowl could have been pulled outside and pushed back in. Reginald, I'm so glad you came. I feel now we might be getting somewhere!" She straightened in her chair, all business.

"Tell me everything that happened Wednesday evening," Rex said spreading jam on a dimpled crumpet. "From the time you put out Archie's food in the conservatory."

"Well, Felicity was here. We were working on an interactive edition for the e-book version of a Claude story. She came with me to the book club afterwards and then drove straight back to London."

"She was with you the whole time?"

"Never out of my sight. We left Madeline's shortly before eight and walked back here, where she picked up her car. I really wish now that I had not gone to the book club!"

Rex knew all about the "if only's." How many times would Patricia recreate in her mind the events of that night so she could have prevented Archie's death?

"You said you usually put out Archie's food at six?"

"That's right. We were running late. I think I must have called him and then left for the book club. Felicity was our guest of honour."

"Did anyone leave during the book club?"

"Leave? No. We were all there until the end."

"No temporary absences?"

"None, apart from the usual bathroom breaks."

"Think hard now," Rex coaxed, hoping against hope his theory was correct.

Patricia screwed up her face in concentration, pushing her lopsided glasses back up her nose with two fingers.

"Take yourself back and recount events in

order as best you can."

"We arrived at the B&B. Madeline greeted us at the door. I introduced Felicity to everyone. Dot, she had already met. Katrina is a young mum with a toddler at home, but she never misses the book club. Says it keeps her sane, although I don't know when she finds the time to read the books. She's married to an architect and lives in one of the converted barns."

Rex grit his teeth, waiting for useful information, yet not wishing to interrupt Patricia's train of thought.

"Jackie writes romantic mysteries and was keen to meet Felicity. They're about the same age, that's to say mid-fifties. They seemed to hit it off, and Jackie was very excited when Felicity agreed to look at some of her work. Then there's Cecilia, who lives in the first cottage you come to in the village. She's well into her nineties, but still likes to garden. And Cheryl. She runs a lunch place in Seaford. Late thirties, married, has a step-son."

Rex was mentally knocking his head against the table by this point.

"That's seven, plus Felicity." Patricia did a count on her fingers. "Yes, all present and accounted for. After wine and hors-d'oeuvres, we discussed the current book, a mystery set in the Shetlands, and then Felicity answered questions about her role as a literary agent and how best to submit, *et cetera*. That's it, really."

"Felicity had read the book you were discussing?"

"Actually, no. She had to take an important call and left us to it. Unless it was a pretext to smoke. She smokes rather more than she should."

"She left the room?"

"I believe so."

"How long was she gone?"

"I'm not sure. Not more than ten or fifteen minutes."

"Enough time to run back to your house. It's only a wee village. Was she wearing heels?"

"Boots, I think. It was windy and raining on Wednesday. Are you suggesting it was Felicity who murdered Archie?"

"At what point did she disappear?"

"We got into the book discussion about half an hour after we arrived."

"Six-thirty?"

"Thereabouts."

Rex sat back in his chair. "Can you remember what else she was wearing on Wednesday?"

"Business attire. Much the same as today, but maybe slacks? She was wearing a red raincoat and had an umbrella. But it wasn't raining when we walked to Madeline's. It felt good to be out, I remember. The air felt very fresh after the rain. I also remember thinking Archie might be out in the garden after being cooped inside all day. His fur always smelled so good after he'd been outdoors." Patricia lost herself in a moment of nostalgia, and then came to again. "But, seriously, Reginald. Felicity can't be your suspect."

"Why not?"

"Because it doesn't make any sense! She made a living off Archie, same as me and Roger, though to a lesser extent."

"Did she ever show Archie any affection?"

"Not especially. She's allergic to cats. Sometimes I had to put him outside the study when she was visiting, as her eyes would start to get irritated." Patricia stared at him through her lenses, her pupils dilated. "That is no reason to get rid of my cat!"

"Well, there's a bit more to it than that. I'm sorry to have to inform you that it was probably her who murdered Archie. Not that anyone on your list would have been good news."

"I never really suspected Felicity. She offered to come when I called her with the news of Archie's death. Felicity Parker? Can you prove it?"

"I have a wee trick up my sleeve. It was on Felicity's sleeve, actually. I picked it off her jacket yesterday when Charles almost knocked her off her feet."

"He can be very clumsy, that boy. But I'm not sure I follow."

"If you could boil the kettle and bring me the Say Goodbye to Archie note and some glue, I'll show you. And I'll need Felicity's home address so I can pay her a personal visit."

*

As Rex got off the train at Victoria Station he wondered if he would catch Felicity at home on a Sunday morning. Yet he felt it unlikely she'd be at church. After all, murdering poor Archie wasn't a very Christian thing to do. Fortunately, she didn't live far away, and if he took a taxi he would have enough time to see her and get to King's Cross for his scheduled train back to Edinburgh.

When he arrived at her address in a nondescript block of flats located in a mainly residential neighbourhood, with an Indian restaurant on the corner, he asked the cabbie to wait while he went to see if the person he was calling on was home. Hoping and praying that she was, he rang on her bell at the front entrance. Felicity's voice answered on the intercom. He gestured to the cabbie that he would be fifteen minutes, and the man nodded and opened a newspaper.

The agent sounded surprised and pleased when he announced himself, and invited him up to her flat. At the door she glanced down at his hands as though expecting flowers. It appeared she had applied a fresh layer of lipstick in the time it had taken him to reach her floor in the lift.

"There's something important I need to

discuss with you," he said, stepping into the narrow hallway.

"Oh. Right. Well, come on through." She led him into a small but comfortable sitting room where stacks of manuscripts bound in elastic bands weighed down a low coffee table. "I brought some work home for the weekend," she explained. "Sometimes I don't get time to read at the office."

"I won't detain you. I have a train to catch, so I'll get straight to the point."

She gave a flirty smile. "Not even time for a drink?"

"Thank you, no."

Felicity indicated for him to take a seat in an armchair and sat facing him on the sofa, leaning forward with her hands in her lap, a blank look on her face. *She knows what I've come to say*, he thought.

"This is not pleasant," he began. "For I have reason to believe you are responsible for the death of your client's cat."

Felicity jumped up, rather like a cat herself. "This is outrageous!"

"Please bear with me while I outline how I came to this conclusion. You will have an opportunity to refute anything I say at the end."

She sat back down with an exaggerated sigh.

"As an agent of not only children's literature, but also of mysteries and gardening books, you would know about the deadly properties of foxglove and, no doubt, reading loads of mysteries would have provided you with a few ideas. Your motive apparently was to silence Patricia's muse and end the Claude series before it deteriorated too far. Sales were down, you told me, and you could generate publicity from the cat's death. Make a killing, so to speak."

He stared Felicity down where she cowered on the sofa vehemently denying everything, her face scarlet between her red hair and pink blouse.

"A newsworthy item," he went on. " 'Beloved Literary Cat's Demise Under Suspicious Circumstances Ignites Indignation and Grief.' Was that the sort of thing?"

"Of course not!"

"Archie's murder was intended as a publicity stunt to garner attention from the legion of Claude fans."

"How could I have carried out his murder?" she demanded.

"You came up from London on Wednesday to discuss some work with Patricia and to attend the book club. You left during the book club on the pretext of an important call and came through Patricia's side gate. The foxglove was readily available in the garden. You used your umbrella to draw the bowl towards you. You mixed the poison with the tuna, and then went on your merry way back to London after the book club. The button yesterday was a red herring when you discovered Patricia suspected foul play. You threw it into the foxglove patch along with the crumbs, thinking to frame Roger. What did you use to cut up the foxglove? Nail scissors?" However, he saw from Felicity's frigid expression that he was not going to get all the answers. "Patricia was no doubt a demanding and eccentric client, and you were stressed," he allowed. "You presumably felt it was preferable to retire the cat and curtail the series rather than terminate your contract with Mrs. Forsyth."

"Those are a lot of conclusions to jump to," the agent scoffed, recovering some of her composure.

"Motive, means and opportunity, Felicity. And I have proof. Your guilty slip yesterday is what made me consider you more closely as a suspect."

"What guilty slip?"

"When you said you never had a chance to say goodbye to Archie."

"So?"

"It was the exact wording that was on the note."

"It's a common enough thing to say, saying goodbye to someone."

Rex looked insistently in her blanched face. "You didn't even ask aboot the note just now. Because you already knew aboot it."

"Patricia told me."

"She did not. You posted it through the front door as a warning. Perhaps you did not intend to kill Archie, just the series. But then something happened to make you snap. And what's more, I have evidence of your guilt."

Felicity licked her dry lips. "What evidence?"

Rex removed the note from its envelope, which he carried in his jacket pocket. "A sample of your hair is stuck behind one of the letters on this note." He peeled back the "G" so she could see. "I don't know anyone else with hair that colour. Not that is doesn't become you," he lied.

Felicity's cheeks looked as though they could melt wax, her mouth frozen in the shape of an "O." Although no words came out, her reaction spoke louder than words.

"In any case, the hair can be forensically proved to belong to you."

"You're going to the police?" she asked in shock.

"That will be up to Patricia. I would think a very public firing at least would be in order. I don't think many authors would want to be represented by an animal killer, do you? Good day to you."

Rex let himself out of the flat.

*

Once he was settled on the train to Edinburgh, he

called Patricia on his mobile. "It's her," he confirmed. "She as good as confessed and fell for the false evidence. I recorded the whole conversation on my phone."

"Oh, goodness. You came through for me, Reginald! I'm so very grateful."

"You can thank Roger. Your illustrator was a fount of information."

"Village life makes gossips of us all."

They discussed suitable retribution for Archie's murder. Nothing was too severe in Patricia's view. "But I think today may be the turning point," she said. "Dr. Strange came by shortly after you left, and you'll never guess what he brought."

"A kitten?"

"You knew!"

"He mentioned it in passing yesterday."

"A little ginger tom. His mother was hit by a car. Dr. Strange was able to save her, but she won't regain her strength for a while. The litter is just about weaned. At first I refused. I thought it would be too soon, but he said the kittens urgently needed homes, so I let him persuade me."

"I think it's a splendid idea."

"Yes, perhaps now that I have some closure, thanks to you... And I've decided to call him Reginald, Reggie for short, in your honour."

Rex found himself speechless for a moment.

But perhaps Reggie wasn't such a bad name for a cat. Rex would suit a dog better. "It is an honour, Patricia," he said. "I'm so glad I could be of help."

After he ended the call, he took out the picture of Archie that she had given him, and smiled. This cat had made an old lady both happy and rich, and was responsible for making long words a hit with short people. How many humans could claim to have achieved more? Aside from the satisfaction of solving the case, he now had a whole new respect for pets of the feline persuasion.

BOOKS IN THE REX GRAVES MYSTERY SERIES:

Christmas Is Murder

Starred Review from *Booklist:*

The first installment in this new mystery series is a winner. The amateur detective is Rex Graves, a Scottish barrister, fond of Sudoku puzzles and Latin quotations. In an old-fashioned conceit, Challinor begins with a cast of characters, along with hints of possible motives for each. Although set firmly in the present, this tale reads like a classic country-house mystery. Rex and the others are snowed in at the Swanmere Manor hotel in East Sussex, England. Being the last to arrive, Rex immediately hears of the unexpected demise of one of the other guests. By the time the police arrive days later, additional bodies have piled up and motives are rampant, but Rex has identified the murderer. At times, it seems we are playing Clue or perhaps enjoying a contemporary retelling of a classic Agatha Christie tale *(And Then There Were None,* or *At Bertram's Hotel)* with a charming new sleuth. A must for cozy fans.

Murder in the Raw

Mystery Scene Magazine:

In *Murder in the Raw*, Scottish barrister Rex Graves must expose—and I do mean expose—the killer of Sabine Durand, a French actress who goes missing one evening from a nudist resort in the Caribbean... Set on an island, *Murder in the Raw* is a clever variant on the locked room mystery, and Rex discovers that everyone in this self-contained locale has a secret when it comes to the intriguing Sabine. Who, though, would benefit from her disappearance or murder? With a host of colorful characters, a dose of humor and a balmy locale, you will want to devour this well-plotted mystery. I won't spoil your pleasure by divulging the solution, but suffice it to say that Challinor provides a most compelling answer.

*Phi Beta Murder**

Foreword Magazine:

Readers meet up once again with Rex Graves in the third mystery to follow the Scottish barrister with a knack for getting involved in the ultimate crime. Rex is on his way out of the beautiful Scottish countryside to visit his son on the campus of his American college. Campbell Graves is supposed to be enjoying life at Hilliard University in Jacksonville, Florida, but lately on the phone he's sounded rather distant, and Rex wants nothing more than to see his son and make sure everything is all right. Unfortunately the day he steps on campus is the day a young man is found in his locked room hanging from the ceiling. Soon Rex must split his time between worrying about his son, solving a crime that seems to involve a million people with a million different agendas, and trying to balance his love life without losing people in the process. Humor and well-written characters add to the story, as does some reflection on the causes of suicide. A wonderful read and great plot for cozy mystery lovers.

Murder on the Moor

BellaOnline:

Scottish Barrister and amateur sleuth Rex Graves purchased Gleneagle Lodge so that he and his girlfriend, Helen D'Arcy, could get away to spend some private time together. Now he wonders why he had agreed to host a housewarming party. When one of the guests turns up dead, her body found in a nearby loch, the finger-pointing begins. Graves cannot help but put his sleuthing skills to work as he tries to find out who killed his house guest while he also gathers clues as to who is committing the so-called Moor Murders. He is wondering if the two are tied and if he is hosting the killer. When a storm prevents anyone from leaving, Rex and Helen do their best to keep everyone calm during their forced confinement. Set in the Scottish Highlands, Challinor successfully utilizes the atmosphere of the countryside to enhance the tension going on inside the Lodge. The characters seem typical of the type seen in many mysteries written by such authors as Agatha Christie, and are a welcome diversion from today's style of writing. The writing is crisp and the story fast-paced. The inevitable gathering of the guests in the library comes with a twist or two, and the ending is a satisfying conclusion to a solid whodunit.

Murder of the Bride

Buried Under Books:

Rex Graves is back, this time visiting his fiancée, Helen d'Arcy, so they can attend the wedding in Aston-on-Trent of one of her former students. Polly Newcombe is very pregnant and her groom, Timmy Thorpe looks a bit peaked, but is it just the dreary day leading Rex to think the success of this marriage is doubtful? Perhaps not, as the reception at the bride's family country home in Derbyshire soon turns from a pleasant celebration to a scene of mayhem when Polly collapses, looking more than a little green. Leaving the reception and heading to Aston-on-Trent, Rex learns a great deal more about the secrets of the Newcombe and Thorpe families. Is jealousy behind the attacks? Greed? Infidelity? Overbearing mothers? Rex and the local police have an overabundance of clues and evidence, and getting to the solution to the case will require much thought and cooperation. This latest case for Rex Graves is every bit as charming and entertaining as those in earlier books and readers will not be disappointed. The setting, an English country home, is as much a character as the people, and many of those characters are a delight (and the cast of characters provided by the author is very much appreciated).

Murder at the Dolphin Inn

Cozy Mystery Book Reviews:

Scottish barrister, Rex Graves, and his fiancée are on a cruise to Mexico. When they disembark at Key West, Florida, they hear of a bizarre story surrounding the local B&B. The owners, Merle and Taffy Dyer, were killed during the Key West's October Fantasy Fest. Rex can't resist a mystery and can't wait to abandon the cruise and dive head first into solving this mystery. It's going to take all of Rex's sleuthing skills to find out who out of all the seemingly innocent family and friends killed the owners. The premise of this mystery reminds me of the traditional mysteries I read in my teens. It is very much reminiscent of M.C. Beaton and Agatha Christie, with a quaint inn and a sleuth determined to find the truth. From their first discovering of the murders to the final revealing of the murderer, Rex and Helen are an outstanding sleuthing duo. They reminded me so much of Agatha Christie's Tommy and Tuppence, hunting down clues and uncovering killers. With numerous twists and turns, *Murder at the Dolphin Inn* provides a first class whodunit, and I absolutely can't wait to find out what adventure Rex and Helen go on next.

ABOUT THE AUTHOR

C.S. Challinor, born in Bloomington, Indiana, was raised and educated in Scotland and England. She now lives in Southwest Florida.

Visit the author at *www.rexgraves.com*.

Made in the USA
Monee, IL
18 January 2024